August

THE GERMAN LIST

CHRISTA WOLF

August

TRANSLATED BY KATY DERBYSHIRE

LONDON NEW YORK CALCUTTA

This publication was supported by a grant
from the Goethe-Institut India

Seagull Books, 2014

First published in English by Seagull Books, 2014

ISBN 978 0 85742 186 9

British Library Cataloguing-in-Publication Data
A catalogue record for this book is available
from the British Library

Typeset in Dante MT Regular by Seagull Books, Calcutta, India

Printed at Hyam Enterprises, Calcutta, India

What can I give you, my dear, if not a few pages of writing, into which a lot of memory has flowed from the time before we knew each other. I can hardly tell you anything about the later times that you don't already know. That's the thing—we've grown together over the years. I can hardly say 'I'—usually 'we'. Without you I'd be a different person. But you know that too. We're not ones for great statements. Only this much—I have been lucky.

C.

28 July 2011

August is remembering. He had been asked when and where he had lost his mother, like all the children who arrived at the train station in Mecklenburg without parents at the end of the war. But he didn't know. And whether the bombing raid on the refugee train happened before or after they crossed the big river they called the Oder. He didn't know that either. He'd been asleep. When the terrible noise started and everyone was screaming, a woman he didn't know, not his mother, had grabbed him by the arm and tugged him out of the train. He threw himself down in the snow behind the embankment with her and lay there until the noise stopped and until the conductor shouted that everyone still alive should get on the train immediately. August never saw his mother or that other woman again. Yes, there were people lying scattered across the field, who didn't get back on the train before it moved on again.

And his father? August didn't think the Red Cross lady was very pretty—grey hair, a wrinkled face, very tired; he could tell by the way she spoke. His father was a soldier. August told her no more than that. His mother had crumpled the letter that had arrived recently in her hand and then she had smoothed it out again, she had cried, he's alive, she'd said, he's alive, I know he is. And Mrs Niedlich, their neighbour, had said the same: Missing doesn't mean dead. But August didn't tell the Red Cross lady that. His father, a man he hardly knew, was alive and would come looking for him, him and the mother he had lost, who wouldn't stop looking for him until she'd found him. He could tell the woman his date of birth though; his mother had practised that with him in case of emergencies. He had just turned eight, then. And he knew the name of his village too. Oh, East Prussia, said the lady. You have come a long way, haven't you? And then she put a card round his neck, and it said 'orphan' along with what he'd told the lady about himself. August sees the card in his mind's eye; he kept it for a long time.

Then he was sent to a doctor in the next room. He was just as tired as the Red Cross lady, and he examined August, listened a long time through his stethoscope and then said: The usual. And that was how he ended up in the castle that called itself a hospital, where all the inmates had one single illness, 'the moths'—consumption—and where he spent a long time. A summer, an autumn and a winter. He knew the seasons, it was just that they were different there than in his village, not as beautiful.

August didn't know the word 'homesickness' and it doesn't occur to him now either, more than sixty years later, as he thinks of the seasons in his village and drives the large tour bus homewards from Prague, concentrated and reliable. This is one of his last trips; he's reached retirement age and more and more often he is accompanied—that's how he'd describe it—by pictures of his village, the one he never saw again. Others, people he knows, have been back many times. He didn't need that; he can see what he wants to see—the elderberry bush clutching at a brick-red wall. The huge, slightly swaying, sun-yellow cornfield. The crowds of blue cornflowers and red poppies on its edges. The changing shapes of clouds in the deep blue sky. The pump outside their house. And it's always summer.

The people from the village still called the hospital 'the manor house' but the patients only ever called it 'consumption castle'. The house's inhabitants had fled, from the Russians, the villagers said, and as everyone had TB after the war, said the head nurse, they had to turn such unsuitable houses into makeshift hospitals. But they couldn't magic up the staff they really needed, said the head nurse. She was a pudgy woman but very quick on her feet and she had eyes everywhere. August didn't notice they had too few staff; he was on the men's ward under Sister Erika, and she had trained her patients to do a lot for themselves. Most of them weren't bedridden, after all, she said. So they could wash themselves, make their beds and sometimes sweep the floor as well. That had never harmed anyone, had it now? Sister Erika had a square face, sunken cheeks and lots of little curls on her head. It's all natural, she said. August thought she had some kind of trouble and sorrow that she didn't want to tell anyone about but it didn't occupy him particularly, because everyone he met at that time had some kind of trouble and sorrow. You have to deal with it on your own, said Mr Grigoleit, the man in the bed opposite August's. He came from East Prussia too and could have been something like his uncle. He had a bushy moustache covering his top lip, which underlined his good nature.

August sees the people he met back then clearly in his mind, more clearly than most people he's come across in his long later life. He remembers Lilo very well indeed, that goes without saying. But he can't remember any more when he first saw her.

It must have been in autumn, it might have been over lunch in the knights' hall, as the patients called the large dining room with pictures of the fled lord of the manor's ancestors still on the walls, the earliest in helmets and chain mail. That was where all the inmates of the manor house met at twelve o'clock sharp for lunch, if you could call what they got served up lunch. That might have been where he first saw Lilo. Which doesn't necessarily mean he noticed her right away. She'll have been sitting with the group from the women's ward next to Ingelore as usual, whom she knew. Small wonder, said the head nurse, that's who she got TB from. They used to sit next to each other at school and put their heads together all the time. And Ingelore's highly contagious, isn't she now? The head nurse liked using medical terminology, and that marked her out from the majority of the manor house inmates, who had about as much idea of medicine as a flock of sparrows. But Lilo doesn't blame Ingelore. It's all just a matter of fate these days. It's no one's fault, is it now?

The handful of children admitted to consumption castle because they had something with the mysterious name of 'hilar tuberculosis'—a disease August never heard of again—sat at the long table between the women's group and the group from the men's ward. August knows he used to sit between Klaus and Ede but he tries in vain to remember what they actually had to eat. It can't have been much, they never felt really full, but at least there was a cook and she must have had potatoes and turnips and carrots and cabbage. There was no fat floating on the soup, though, and he doubts there was ever any meat.

The first time he noticed Lilo was when she had an argument with the head nurse. She wanted to forbid the women on the women's ward from toasting their dry slices of bread on the little stove by the front wall of the large room. Lilo saw no sense to this rule; she thought it was over the top and she told the head nurse so. The head nurse was responsible for order and safety in all the rooms, but Lilo said you could only eat the soggy slices of bread if they were toasted. No need to mention there was no butter to put on them, or that the ration of turnip jam was all gone by the end of breakfast. But still! said the head nurse, and Lilo simply turned on her heel and went into the women's ward. The bread went on being toasted and August had watched the whole performance from the doorway of the men's ward, which was in the corridor opposite the door of the women's ward. It hadn't occurred to him that any one could contradict the head nurse until that point.

August thought Lilo was beautiful and he still thinks so now, on his driving seat in the tourist bus, transporting a group of jolly pensioners from Prague to Berlin. They don't want to hear a word of what the tour guide, Mrs Richter, has to say about the Elbe Sandstone Mountains; they want to compare the bargain souvenirs they bought in Prague and then they want to sing. Mr Walter calls the tunes, even standing up in the front row, turning round and conducting the choir, which sings 'On the Lüneburg Heath' in full voice. August prefers quiet on his bus; he likes it best when the passengers are asleep. He's very fond of the road running alongside the River Elbe, in every season and every light. The singers behind him see nothing of it. He exchanges glances with Mrs Richter, with whom he often does tours. She shrugs and falls back onto her seat. She doesn't need the microphone any more.

Lilo used to like singing too; there was often singing from the women's ward. August remembers sneaking into the women's ward for the first time, his heart thudding and then, when no one sent him out, taking a seat on the chair by the stove and listening to the singing as if it were the most natural thing in the world. Sometimes Ilse, the student nurse, would stand next to him and listen too, and sometimes she'd sing along when Lilo struck up a folk song, 'If you want to walk with joy' for instance. August still knows the words but he's never sung again since those days. Where would he sing and who with? Trude was not a great singer. But he'll never forget how Lilo came past him after the singing and spoke to him: Ah, I bet you like music, eh? And how she asked him what his name was after that, and how he had to tell her his name: August. And how she repeated his name and it sounded quite different from when anyone else spoke it out loud, and how very much he liked hearing his name when she said it. For from that day on he was stuck on her.

Stuck himself to her, you might say, and he didn't care if she noticed it or even wanted it in the first place—he did what he had to do.

Winter came and the consumption castle turned into an ice palace. The head nurse didn't stop accusing the authorities of having dumped lung-disease patients in a marshland where poisonous vapours came out of the ground in autumn, and of apparently intending to let them all freeze to death now it was winter. She forced the old doctor—who came over from Boltenhagen once a week to X-ray the important cases and give the most important ones pneumothorax treatments—to listen to her complaints as they walked down the long corridor to the consulting room. She told him the climate here inevitably led to colds, which only added to the primary infection for which they were all here and, as the doctor wouldn't deny, often enough had disastrous consequences. The doctor didn't deny it, he didn't deny anything, he admitted that a little more fat would foster the improvement of the lung disease; it was just that the head nurse couldn't tell him where she was to get the fat either. There was none, not a year after the end of the war, not for healthy people and not for sick people. Then the head nurse pursed her lips and called the candidates scheduled for X-rays one at a time into the consulting room, in the middle of which was the machine, which they had to nestle up to with their torsos bared, whereupon the doctor looked at the green-glowing inner image of their body from the other side of the glass and dictated what he saw to the head nurse. In Lilo's case he saw an infiltrate in the right third ICS, towards which he was rather favourably disposed because it did not develop into a cavern over the weeks, as was unfortunately frequently the case with other patients. In Gabi's case, for instance, Lilo's closest friend along with Ingelore. Gabi was thin, a real skinny-malinky, the head nurse said disapprovingly, and consequently the harmless opacity with which she'd been admitted had developed exceedingly quickly into the cavity, which Gabi was not to know about. But Lilo knew all about it. Because of the lack of staff in the consumption castle she had been promoted to a kind of assistant nurse. It was her responsibility to read off and note down the results of the blood sedimentation tests in the tubes at the stipulated intervals, test tubes lined up in a wooden rack in the head nurse's office, which provided the doctors with important indications for their diagnoses. As August wanted to know everything that had anything to do with Lilo, he granted her not a minute's peace until she gave him a basic introduction to the secrets of blood sedimentation. The level of the red blood cells in the measurement tube was measured at certain intervals, and the higher the level was, the worse. All the better if the level, like in her own case, didn't go above ten; that was just ideal, said the head nurse. But that meant she couldn't prevent Lilo from knowing how serious the other patients' results were. Not knowing any other way to deal with it, the head nurse made her swear a vow of silence, which she stuck to. August fully appreciated and greatly respected that. Lilo could never behave in anything but an exemplary manner.

So not a word to Gabi about her blood sedimentation or about how the old doctor had refused to give her a pneu, which meant something like pumping her lung up with air and squeezing the wormy spots—that was what the head nurse called them—so that the consumption moths lost their habitat. Gabi didn't ask after the treatment, unlike most of the patients. Gabi was a cheery old fellow, that was what the head nurse called her. And it was true. Gales of laughter often came bursting across the women's ward from the corner where Lilo, Ingelore and Gabi lay next to each other during their rest cure. Not everyone liked that. Miss Schnell, for instance, who sat in her bed bearing down upon her rampant growth of chin hairs with a pair of tweezers, found the three friends' behaviour simply inconsiderate. She's just envious because she hasn't any friends, said Gabi.

Gabi had no one, by the way, as August found out bit by bit; she was all alone in the world just like him. He heard it from Gabi herself when he was sitting on his little chair in the women's ward, as he so often did, sneaking in more and more often until no one even noticed he was there or thought of sending him out. Gabi's mother had died, then, after they came West. Of the moths too, of course, in a different hospital where Gabi had been on the same ward as Lilo before. Where Lilo had already found out what August listened in to now, that Gabi and her mother had had to bed down in a miserable lodging room run by a witch of a landlady. Where they hadn't even been able to wash properly. That detail had stuck in August's mind, and it occurs to him as he drives his bus into the outskirts of Dresden. Now that they're supposed to get off soon, the pensioners are asleep behind him; he's used to that.

We could wash in the consumption castle, he thinks, if only with cold water. It'll toughen you up, the head nurse used to say, and he can see her now, and the dingy washroom with the defective wash-basins. He didn't have a bathroom of his own for a long time after the war; first came the years in the children's home, which he doesn't like to think of, then his apprenticeship as a mechanic in a state firm, living in the apprentices' home, communal shower rooms all those years—August wasn't used to anything else.

He still remembers what a lucky coincidence it was that he had to stand in as a co-driver in a company truck one day, when a workmate had fallen ill.

And how much he enjoyed driving across country. It was the first time he'd enjoyed something; he hasn't forgotten that. And it was the first time he'd wanted something. He wanted to be a truck driver. For the first time, he didn't wait to see what other people wanted him to do. He went to the personnel department of his own accord. He can still picture his colleague flicking through his personnel file, hesitating. Well, driving was a very responsible job of course. I know that, said August, who otherwise rarely opened his mouth. Well, the firm did have its own driving school of course, August knew that too, but the next course was fully booked; perhaps if someone dropped out. August went to the personnel department every day and asked if anyone had dropped out, and one day, shortly before the new course started, his colleague waved the certificate at him, already filled out in his name and entitling him to take part in the driving course and then to drive a heavy goods vehicle. August was unpractised at joy; it was an unfamiliar feeling. He has thought of it often recently.

August still remembers the face Lilo made when Gabi wasn't allowed to take part in communal mealtimes any more. It was only temporary, she said to Gabi, and she called Sister Ilse as her witness, who brought Gabi's meals to her in bed from then on. Ilse gave an anxious nod, but outside the door August heard her say to Lilo, in an almost punishing tone: With her blood sedimentation! As if Lilo were to blame for Gabi's blood sedimentation. Lilo though, instead of going to the dining room herself, went back to Gabi and tried to shove as much as possible from her plate into her mouth, because Gabi had started refusing her food. Lilo could be very gentle but then suddenly turn very tough; August heard that. Gabi ought to just think of how many people would be glad of a plate of lunch like that nowadays. Who liked eating swede every day? But she ought to just imagine it was buttered potatoes with peas, or whatever else she liked eating. Rice pudding with sugar and cinnamon and melted butter, said Gabi, almost shocked, and Lilo said: There you are then. And went on feeding her. And then they sang a little and Gabi sang her favourite song: 'Oh, my dad is a beautiful clown, Oh, my dad is a really great artist.' And when Lilo came out of the ward with the plate you might have thought she was crying, then she dropped the plate on the stone stairs by accident and August helped her to gather up the shards. You're always nearby, aren't you? Lilo said to August then, and he nodded.

She seemed to like it. The women on the women's ward started joking about the two of them: Lilo was the princess and August must be her page. August didn't know what a page was but when Lilo asked him he remembered the Sleeping Beauty fairy tale his mother had once read to him. He could barely remember his mother's face but all at once he clearly saw her hands holding the book. Lilo didn't need a book; she told the story by heart, in the children's corner of the men's ward before they went to sleep at night. That was the most wonderful thing August could imagine, except that he had to share that most wonderful experience with the other children, with Klaus and Anneliese and with Ede. And except that Lilo went to each child's bed afterwards and wished them all goodnight, not just him. Even though he was certain she belonged to him. But he had to see, Lilo reminded him, that Klaus and

Anneliese—whose mother Mrs Wittkowski was on the small women's ward, where the severe cases were tacitly housed—also had a right to a goodnight song, and Ede certainly did too. Ede hadn't even known what his name was when they fished him out of a group of refugees where no one knew him. Or wanted to know him. Ede was a wild, unpredictable child, that was what the head nurse said. Not easy to like. He didn't have a date of birth or a place of origin or a surname. When they gave him a pencil and paper he scribbled down EDE, so perhaps he'd been sent to school for a couple of months. They gave him the surname of foundling—Ede Findling they'd called him, and it suited him.

He's not right in the head, said the head nurse, he belongs somewhere else entirely. But Lilo said it wasn't that he wasn't right in the head. He'd been damaged by something he'd experienced, which was too much for him. That's why he'd forgotten everything. Ede attacked everyone for no reason, hit and scratched and spat, and two men had to hold him down.

He lay still during the goodnight song. When Lilo went to say goodnight to him, he turned away. August couldn't stand Ede but it was out of the question for Lilo to favour him over other children. He could put his mind at ease about that. It was worse with Little Hannelore, in every sense. Little

Hannelore was no more than five years old. She'd had papers on her, a pouch round her neck with papers, when they found her. And there was a letter her mother had written, addressed to an unknown good soul who'd find Hannelore if anything happened to her mother. That good soul, she wrote, should take care of the child and God would see to a reward.

August doesn't like the outskirts of cities. The huge, ugly shopping centres with their oversized car parks. The car showrooms outbidding each other's advertising claims. The fast-food restaurants that August never sets foot inside. He usually brings his own sandwiches along, although they're not as lovingly made as when Trude was alive. He's not hungry yet. He has to concentrate on the motorway near the city, which gets more and more crowded with every year, on the building sites that never end, only change position. On the traffic jams they cause, which make the journey longer. August keeps his cool. He never gets impatient. You have the patience of an angel, Trude used to tell him. He never loses his temper. His workmates appreciate that. Sometimes, he knows, they think he's a bit boring. Come on, say something for a change, they used to nudge him in the beginning when they sat together in their lunch break. But what did he have to say? He had no reason to complain about his wife. No separation to report on. No arguments with the children to moan about. They didn't have any children. It had simply turned out that way. There'd been no need to talk to Trude about it first. They wanted for nothing. And when Trude died two years ago he certainly couldn't talk to anyone about it.

Little Hannelore had the smallest room to herself and everyone accepted that. No matter how candidly and endlessly they discussed their own progress, their results, their possible discharge dates, they never mentioned Little Hannelore. As if she didn't exist. The only person who had to make an exception was Lilo, of course. August didn't like it one bit when Lilo went into Hannelore's room. He knew she sang songs for her or read stories. And he knew he wasn't allowed to sneak in with her. It went on that way for a while until one day the head nurse called Lilo out of the room, in the middle of the lovely song 'The moon has risen,' and no, she wasn't allowed to finish the song, she had to come out to the corridor and listen to the head nurse telling her to stop her visits to Hannelore immediately. Did she not know how severely ill the child was, how infectious?

And did she want to get herself a new infection?

No, Lilo didn't want that. But she couldn't just stay away from Little Hannelore now; what would she think? She'd stand by the door, she wouldn't go close to Hannelore's bed, where the moths no doubt swarmed in thick clouds. And that was what Lilo did, no matter what the head nurse said. You know what Little Hannelore's favourite catch-phrase is? Lilo asked them one afternoon. 'What's up? Three candies in a cup.' But they didn't even have three candies for her. When Lilo said goodbye to her, she'd say: 'Here's mud in your eye, magpie.' Her mother must have been a funny old jug, said the head nurse. Soon Sister Ilse refused to draw blood from Little Hannelore, and Sister Erika declared herself incapable of inserting a needle into her thin wee arm. So Lilo couldn't read off Hannelore's latest blood sedimentation, but that was hardly necessary now anyway. That's what Harry said to Lilo. She wasn't well pleased by that. But she still went out walking with Harry.

Dresden. August knew the city as a ruin. He's seen all the stages of its reconstruction and he likes it here. He knows the best way to get to the city centre, where to park when he's dropped the passengers off at the 'Italian Village', where they insist on going for a meal. They invite him to join them but he turns them down. He gets himself a sausage at a stall and strolls over to the Frauenkirche. He goes to look at the church every time he's in Dresden.

He didn't believe they could rebuild it, and he's touched now that it's almost complete. He's not a religious man; Trude and he never went to church, didn't have a church wedding either. The registrar was rather austere but afterwards they had a glass of sparkling wine in a good restaurant, for the first time in their lives, and they were in a good mood, almost ceremonial. August takes it as consolation that the church is being built up again here, although he couldn't say for what. And when he stands on Brühl's Terrace and watches the clouds mounted up above the Elbe, he feels comforted.

The bus starts off again on time. Every time he passes the Spreewald junction, August thinks of the lovely time Trude and he once had in the Spreewald forest. They never travelled much—he didn't want to be driving in his holidays and Trude liked to stay in one place. The memories of the few trips have stuck in his mind all the more. They usually spent their holidays on their balcony, which Trude had lovingly transformed into an oasis of blossoms. When they sat there drinking coffee in the afternoon and eating home-baked cake and he showed her how satisfied he was, she might have said he really didn't ask much. He's had a good life; no one can tell him otherwise. August doesn't know whether he's changed since he was a child but he remembers very well that Lilo once said to him: You can't get enough, can you?

It was true. No matter what she did, whether she sang to the children, told fairy tales or recited poems, August couldn't get enough. He begged and pleaded her to recite his favourite poem again so he could again feel that shudder at the last line: 'The child in his arms finds he motionless, dead.' Anneliese and Klaus preferred the poem about the sorcerer's apprentice. They acted it out and even Ede joined in when they pretended to be the floods of water. One evening, however, a new poem surpassed everything Lilo had recited before, and August repeated the storyline to himself until late at night. He didn't know what a tyrant was but he'd understood that one friend was prepared to risk his life for another friend. Gruesome lines that August soon knew by heart: 'I boast one friend whose life for mine, If I should fail the cross, is thine.' He had never felt such fear as for that friend's life, nor such happiness as when it was saved by his friend's loyalty. The next day, he went to Lilo and asked her: Are we friends? And she stroked his head and said: Yes.

And yet she went out walking with Harry, and August suffered from the suspicion that he might be her friend as well. All through the inhospitable, cold, rainy autumn, they strode round the neglected grounds, talking. What did Lilo have to talk about with that Harry, who certainly wasn't handsome with his wavy fair hair and his hump of a nose, who was always twisting his lips because he was always ridiculing everything and who couldn't talk without waving his arms about. Lilo looked askance at him but she did listen to what he said.

August can't remember the sun ever shining that autumn. The wind was always blowing rain against the windowpanes, rotten branches came crashing down from the trees, which grew bare early in the year, and large puddles formed in the marshy spots round the castle. It was one big disaster, said the head nurse, and anyone who sent lung-disease patients to a place like this ought to be punished. She said it straight out to the young lady doctor on her rounds but the doctor only shrugged her shoulders. Where were the authorities supposed to put all the sick?

You were lucky enough if the lady doctor came on her rounds at all, by the way. If she didn't spend all day holed up in the room she lived in at the top of the house, hungover from the previous night's debaucheries. All words that August heard for the first time from the head nurse, which gave the children plenty to gossip about amongst themselves. What they'd seen for themselves early one morning was the lady doctor vomiting over the balustrade of the balcony over the dining hall, where she'd held one of her parties overnight, not without a great deal of noise. She didn't know the meaning of consideration, in the head nurse's opinion. The teacher from the village came regularly, the pharmacist from the town, a few good-for-nothing individuals washed up here by the end of the war. Where they got the alcohol they consumed in generous amounts, only dear God alone knew.

She wasn't ugly, by the way, the lady doctor, with her long dark hair, her slim figure and her green eyes. No wonder she attracted men like a honeypot lures bees. And it may well have been that she had to make up for the youth the war had spoilt for her. It was just that she wasn't cut out for medicine. She'd scurry round the wards, couldn't remember the patients' names even if they'd been there long and she certainly didn't know their symptoms. She'd flick nervously through the medical files when the old doctor from Boltenhagen wanted to know something, and the patients found it amusing that the head nurse, who knew all their cases precisely, held her tongue and didn't even think of helping her out. It was her with whom the doctor consulted as to whether a patient should get pneumothorax treatment. They could discuss that endlessly on the wards, because of course the experienced patients had long since formed their own opinions on how everyone ought to be treated. And they knew what it meant when the doctor didn't grant a pneu even though a person's cavity had enlarged, for the sickness sometimes simply reached a stage when there was nothing more to be done.

There was no medicine, except perhaps with the Americans in the West, and there was no fat either, the only thing that could help. And by the way, Miss Schnell on the women's ward happened to know that badger grease was said to work wonders, but where on earth were they to get badger grease? And from the men's ward came the information that there were some who'd healed themselves by drinking their own urine.

But some simply died. It was never announced; none of the nurses ever said a word. A strange silence came over the place, never to be heard otherwise.

There were always some who'd seen precisely that person's death coming but even they fell silent for a while, though for not more than a day. Until the coffin was out of the house. The inhabitants found out when that was with infallible certainty, from a never fathomed source. At the appointed hour they would gather at the windows facing the rear exit. There stood the two-wheeled cart lined with black fabric, with which the coffin was to be transported to the small chapel in the grounds. By the cart stood the men who would push it—Karle the janitor and two or three patients from the men's ward. August noticed that Harry was always among them. But all everyone wanted to see was the coffin—whether the body was carried out of the house head-first or feet-first. If they carried it out head-first, you see, another dead body would soon follow it, in its footsteps, so to speak. That was vouched for.

Of course, the children weren't supposed to be party to all that. They'd always be chased away but they saw and heard everything and they whispered about it amongst themselves. August, who has to take a break at the pensioners' request, stretching his legs on the edge of a sparse pine wood, can envisage it all, as if it were a film. Even though he's forgotten so many other things, because they weren't worth holding on to, he thinks. What has he ever experienced? Apart from everything to do with Trude; he remembers all that as if it were yesterday. Her behind the till in her white coat at the state retail outlet that stayed open longer than the other shops. Him always shopping there after his shift ended. Her recognizing him and starting to say hello. Her helping him to put his shopping in the bag because he was clumsy at it. Both of them leaving the shop at the same time one day and her walking a little way with him because they'd noticed they both lived in the same direction. Neither of them was married. Trude was a year older. Once she came up with him because he had no idea how to cook the meal for which she'd sold him the ingredients. So she made the meatballs for the two of them, they ate together, the meal was wonderful but that was all. Well, what else would anyone expect, thought August, and he still thinks so now.

Back on the road. The pensioners have perked up. They're now approaching the area round Bestensee, where Trude was born and grew up. The pensioners feel like singing again and almost all of them know 'Little Ann of Tharau', as does August. It occurs to him that he's hardly ever sung since his time at the sanatorium, where the children used to sing along with Lilo. A grown man doesn't sing when he's not drunk. Trude sometimes used to hum a tune in the kitchen and she'd sing quietly too—'Why are you weeping, florist dear?' or 'Three lilies, three lilies, I planted on my grave.' August had always liked that because then he knew Trude was in a good mood.

When they carried Gabi's coffin out in November, Lilo walked with it to the chapel in the pouring rain. Then she was gone all day long, no matter how hard August looked for her. You give her a bit of peace today, my lad, said the head nurse to him in passing, and August holed himself up in his bed and Mr Grigoleit said: Death is a very cruel judge.

Yet that death did have one good effect, although that wasn't something you were supposed to think, August did know that. Lilo stopped going out walking with Harry, and when Harry waylaid her in the grounds she turned round and left him standing, while August was allowed to go with her. Everyone was talking about it and, of course, August found out what had happened too. There was a test of courage in the consumption castle—during the first night when a fresh corpse was laid out in the chapel, the bravest of the brave had to sneak into the chapel at midnight and touch the coffin. At least one witness had to be there, and the next day the bold hero would brag of his daring deed. Harry, who was always looking for an opportunity to show off, informed his closest friends and also Lilo that it'd be him who'd touch Gabi's coffin that night. Lilo forbade him from doing so. Harry, however, couldn't make a fool of himself in front of his friends and did what he'd announced, with witnesses. And they made sure all the patients in the consumption castle found out about it the next day. Lilo, apparently, didn't say a word, but she stopped speaking to Harry and certainly didn't go out walking with him any more. It was a desecration of a grave, for her, said Mr Grigoleit. And he called Harry callous.

August's bus is now passing through the outskirts of Berlin, where the traffic grows dense and confusing. This is a job for younger drivers, he thinks every time. He has to concentrate hard although he's getting tired by now. Sludgy weather, he thinks, grey on grey. Typical Berlin weather. But he's not really serious; he and Trude would never have wanted to live in any town but Berlin. Even though he was actually a farmer, if you asked Trude anyway, a man who belonged in the countryside. He didn't mind her saying that, and now he remembers Lilo calling him 'my little farmer' once too. That was when he brought her a handful of overlooked potatoes he'd dug up from a neighbouring field, which they cooked and ate in secret one evening after the kitchen ladies had gone home. That was perhaps the most wonderful thing August experienced with Lilo. In return, she sometimes gave him some of the beet molasses her father had brought her one day in a pail. He had just come out of a prisoner-of-war camp and tracked down his family living in a barn in a Mecklenburg village. Lilo knew, and told August, how the molasses was made with hours of stirring, in the scullery belonging to the farmers who had given Lilo's family a roof over their heads as refugees from the East. She had a whole cup of molasses every afternoon. At last she's putting on weight, said the head nurse. That sticky stuff might just save her life.

Little Hannelore died though, at Christmas of all times. Lilo had visited her in her last few days, no matter what the head nurse had to say. She said perhaps some people had a guardian angel, and August was convinced Lilo was one of those people. When Hannelore's little coffin was carried out, the patients who were allowed to get out of bed gathered in the hall and sang 'Silent Night'. And Mr Grigoleit said: What the Lord loves he takes for Himself. Lilo snapped at him for that: The Lord wasn't a robber. There was no report of whether anyone was daring enough to sneak into the chapel at midnight to touch Little Hannelore's coffin. But to this day August is convinced none of the patients would have been so callous as to insult a little dead girl.

August remembers that Lilo didn't sing the children a goodnight song on the evening after Hannelore died. Mutely, she sat on his bed as usual and he asked her, quietly so the others didn't hear: Are you sad? And Lilo said quietly: Yes. And August felt, and he feels it to this day, that he'd never get closer to Lilo than at that moment, and he learnt that grief and happiness can be mixed with one another. As he drives towards Alexanderplatz he wonders whether he had another example of that lesson in his later life. He can't think of any. Perhaps he learnt the most important thing for his whole life that early on, with the aid of a person for whom he felt something he couldn't put into words. Even now, so many years later, he'd never say the word for it, not even in his mind. Nor would he think of calling himself 'timid'; it has never occurred to him to think about himself.

It was enough that Trude sometimes looked at him in a certain way that told him she knew what he was like. He remembers now how she once summed up how she saw him—it was when she asked if they didn't want to get married. I think you're a decent person, she'd said. That one sentence lasted all the years of their marriage.

Once he overheard one of his workmates saying, about him, that he wasn't all that bright. It didn't bother him. He knew that about himself anyway. Lilo had told him, after they'd spent the first few lessons together: August, you're not a school person. The village that the manor house belonged to had no space left because of all the refugees, so they had set up a classroom in the manor house where the young, hastily trained teacher could give lessons to the children from the village and the ones from the consumption castle. The teacher's name was Mr Bauer and actually he still looked like a schoolboy himself, August thought. He rather took to the young teacher. Unfortunately, Lilo seemed to take to him as well, or at least she almost always stayed in the classroom during lessons and helped Mr Bauer with his teaching when he needed it. August heard her addressing the teacher by his first name, Rainer, and he didn't like that one bit. When had Lilo found out his first name? And did the teacher call Lilo by her first name too?

August had to admit, though, that Lilo's help was often really necessary during lessons. Most of the children were from refugee families and hadn't seen a school from the inside for a long time. Absolutely neglected, was what the head nurse called them when they ran rampant up and down the staircase and when they threw wet balls of paper torn out of their exercise books off the terrace on the first floor, which was in front of the classroom. They had no mind for how hard it was to get hold of an exercise book in the first place. They're little savages, said the head nurse, they're hopeless cases. August didn't take part in their outrages, of course. Klaus and Anneliese, the other children from the consumption castle, were just as restrained but Ede could lose his temper at the drop of a hat, so badly that Mr Bauer and Lilo could barely calm him down. It was no surprise that he was among the worst of all the very poor pupils. But whereas August said nothing when his name was called, never knowing the answer, Ede thought up cheeky answers and insisted on them defiantly. One day Mr Bauer handed out the exercise books with the dictation test they'd sat for a few days before. He called the results 'exceedingly sad' and indeed he seemed to be saddened by them. August's page was almost entirely covered in red ink, and Lilo shrugged in resignation when she handed it to him. The truth was that he had hardly written one of the simple words correctly and the E grade at the bottom of the page was unfortunately justified. The teacher had given Ede an F, however, and when he saw that he burst into a howl of rage, grabbed his book and ran out onto the terrace, where he clambered onto the low brick wall and threatened to jump. The class suddenly fell silent, apart from Klaus saying: He'll do it.

August saw that Mr Bauer had gone very pale and that Lilo was running to the terrace door, and he heard her calling out to Ede. A grade for a test wasn't so important that he had to jump out of the window, she told him. Ede yelled back that he was always the worst of all, no one liked him and he'd had about enough of it. I'm going to jump! he threatened at the top of his voice. August saw Lilo approaching Ede with tiny steps, talking insistently to him in that tone of hers that August so loved. Didn't he think she liked him? And couldn't he imagine how sad she'd be if he jumped? And there were so many nice things they could do together.

Ede seemed to be listening but to cover up for it he kept shouting: I'm going to jump! and he slung his exercise book over the balustrade. That doesn't matter, Lilo said gently, I'll give you a new one with all the right words in it. I'm going to jump!—

I know you want to, said Lilo, but if I ask you, couldn't you stay here with us for my sake? She'd got very close to Ede, so close that she was next to him in one step and pulled him down from the balustrade in an embrace. For a little while they remained in that embrace and then Lilo put her arm round Ede's shoulder and led him back to his place in the classroom. August saw her giving Mr Bauer a sign not to say anything and he saw him understand and continue the lesson as if nothing had happened. And he noticed how quiet the class was for the rest of the lesson.

It has been getting darker and darker since they drove into Berlin. August has to turn on the lights, and long lines of double headlights bear down on him from the oncoming lane. He's begun to get tired at this time of day; he asks Mrs Richter to pour him a coffee from his thermos flask, and he drinks. It does him good. They're already driving past Ostbahnhof station, fully refurbished. He exchanges a few words with Mrs Richter, about their passengers, who they can't complain about, about the weather. There might be snow later on. You had to reckon with that in November. You always reckon with everything, says Mrs Richter, who knows August pretty well. And he knows about her difficult relationship with her unfaithful partner, whom she loves all the same. August doesn't understand it but he doesn't pass judgement, and he listens attentively when Mrs Richter needs to get it off her chest. No one else is such a good listener as he is, she says.

He never turned out an ace at writing, even though Lilo practised spelling with him and Ede in the afternoons. He did look forward to those times, when Lilo devoted her attention to him, but it annoyed him that Ede was there too. Ede never felt like learning anything and hardly got anywhere, while August made modest progress, later getting steady Ds for dictation at proper school. He was good at reading though; Lilo often praised him for that. True, there was no comparison to Klaus and

Anneliese. They were blond and blue-eyed and lively and everyone liked them, they got good grades from Mr Bauer and they had their mother there too. She was in the small women's ward, and the children were only really there because of their mother and because no one knew where else to put them. That's what August heard the head nurse telling Lilo, who seemed to know why Klaus and Anneliese's mother was on the small women's ward, which was otherwise reserved for the severe cases. No no, said the head nurse, you couldn't keep them that strictly apart, what with the shortage of beds. The old doctor from Boltenhagen had refused to give Klaus and Anneliese's mother a pneumothorax, nonetheless.

August remembers that Trude always took care of everything involving writing in their marriage. If I die before you, she used to say, you'll have to get yourself a guardian. Now it's an effort to struggle through the small amount of correspondence he has to deal with. Fortunately, he has a neighbour who works at the job centre and helps him out when it gets too much for him. In fact, he's always come across helpful people when he's needed them, August thinks. But the list of his friends he recites now in his mind is not long. He avoided the drinking evenings where his workmates met up but sometimes they'd go along on group outings, Trude and him. Once they went down the Danube from Vienna to Passau; he admired the ship's fittings a great deal.

And now the first snowflakes start to fall, and the wind drives them past the windows. The passengers at the back say St Peter could at least have waited until they got home. The snowfall grows thicker very quickly; August has to switch the windscreen wipers to fast or they wouldn't cope with the onslaught. But there are only a few hundred metres left to go now.

The bus stop is outside the travel agency on Alexanderplatz. The passengers have to get out in the snow. August helps the disabled ones with their luggage. He turns down the tips some of them want to give him but he accepts their thanks. Mrs Richter and he wave goodbye to each other. August has to drive the bus to the garage at the bus station. He hands it over to the mechanic, who asks him about technical problems. There weren't any, he says. OK, says his workmate. He seems to trust August's judgement.

His old VW is parked next to the bus station, covered in snow. August has to free it from the wet layer before he can get in and drive off, lining up in the heavy rush-hour traffic heading east, a route he could take in his sleep. It will take him longer than usual today; lots of drivers have trouble with the slippery road surfaces, blocking the way or causing obstructions. In this weather, at this time of day, the city is dirty and forbidding.

Just as the castle and its surroundings were depressing in similar weather; that was how the head nurse put it. It's enough to drive anyone round the bend, she said. It's no wonder people are dying on us, it's because they lose their will to live in all this gloom. It was weather like this, August knows perfectly well still, when Klaus and Anneliese's mother died. The coffin bearers carried her carelessly head-first out of the house and had to struggle through the driving snow to the chapel, and probably no one went out at midnight to touch the coffin, not in that God-awful weather. Or at least that was what Mr Grigoleit said, consoling Klaus and Anneliese. Time heals all wounds, he said, and they were so young still, they had their whole lives ahead of them and there was a good reason why God gave us the power to forget. There was one thing they ought to know, though: There was no way on earth that their mother would pass up to heaven without bidding farewell to her children first. They should pay close attention to what happened on the third night after her death.

On the third night, at the midnight hour, there were three dull thuds against the foot of Klaus and

Anneliese's beds. Mr Grigoleit was most satisfied. Now she's bid her farewells, he said. Now you must let her pass in peace.

The head nurse put her hands to her head but she said nothing, and Lilo said nothing either, although August could see very well she was angry. He realizes he can flick through these old stories like through a picture book, nothing forgotten, no picture faded. Whenever he wants, he can see it all in his mind's eye—the inside of the castle, the broad curved staircase, every single room, the way the beds were arranged on the ward where Lilo was. Since Gabi had been gone there was no more singing there; since Klaus and Anneliese had been put into a children's home it was no more fun when Lilo told a story or sang a song only for him and Ede. It was no fun for her either, August could tell. Towards the beginning of spring, Ingelore was discharged as well. She wasn't cured but her parents were moving away and they took her with them. And August's heart clenched when he heard the head nurse telling Lilo her blood sedimentation was absolutely normal now, just like a healthy young woman. He could work out what that meant.

August has arrived in his suburb of Marzahn. He's lived here for more than twenty years now; he likes it and he wouldn't think of moving away like many of his neighbours. Bedroom, living room, kitchen, bathroom—it was enough for the two of them, Trude and him. Their little balcony. And the view from the kitchen window across a broad swathe of land up to the edge of the woods. He knows where he can park his car. He knows every step in the stairwell up to the second floor, where he lives.

Lilo gave him her address when she said goodbye. He told her not to forget him. I won't, she said and she hugged him. I won't forget you, August. The juddering ambulance that had delivered new patients gave her a lift to the train station. The last he saw of her was her arm, waving out of the side window with the blue scarf she always used to wear. And August thought there'd be no more joy for the rest of his life.

He puts the key in the lock of his front door. It's not good coming home to an empty flat. You get used to it, they'd said when Trude died. August hasn't got used to it. Every time it's an effort, opening the front door when he comes back from work. Every time he's afraid of the silence that will envelop him, something no radio and no television can dispel.

He allows himself a little breather. He's still not capable of putting what he feels into words. He feels something like gratitude that there was something in his life that, if he could express it, he'd call happiness. He pushes open the front door and goes inside.